How the Alphabet was Made

Rudyard Kipling
Illustrated by Chloë Cheese

PETER BEDRICK BOOKS
NEW YORK

First American edition published in 1987 by Peter Bedrick Books 125 East
23 Street New York, NY 10010. Published by agreement with Macmillan
Children's Books, a division of Macmillan Publishers Ltd., London &
Basingstoke.

Text copyright The National Trust

Illustrations copyright © 1983 Macmillan Publishers Ltd.

Library of Congress Cataloging-in-Publication Data
    Kipling, Rudyard, 1865–1936.
        How the alphabet was made.

    (A Just so story)
    Summary: While on a fishing trip, a cave man and his daughter
devise the first written alphabet.
        [1. Alphabet—Fiction. 2. Cave dwellers—Fiction] I. Cheese, Cloë,
ill. II. Title. III. Series: Kipling, Rudyard, 1865–1936. Just so stories.
PZ7.K632Hd   1987   [E]   86–28881
    ISBN 0-87226-136-0 (lib. bdg.)

Printed in Hong Kong
Reinforced binding

 THE week after Taffimai Metallumai (we will still call her Taffy, Best Beloved) made that little mistake about her Daddy's spear and the Stranger-man and the picture-letter and all, she went carp-fishing again with her Daddy. Her Mummy wanted her to stay at home and help hang up hides to dry on the big drying-poles outside their Neolithic Cave, but Taffy slipped away down to her Daddy quite early, and they fished. Presently she began to giggle, and her Daddy said, 'Don't be silly, child.'

'But wasn't it inciting!' said Taffy. 'Don't you remember how the Head Chief puffed out his cheeks, and how funny the nice Stranger-man looked with the mud in his hair?'

'Well do I,' said Tegumai. 'I had to pay two deerskins—soft ones with fringes—to the Stranger-man for the things we did to him.'

'*We* didn't do anything,' said Taffy. 'It was Mummy and the other Neolithic ladies—and the mud.'

'We won't talk about that,' said her Daddy. 'Let's have lunch.'

Taffy took a marrow-bone and sat mousy-quiet for ten whole minutes, while her Daddy scratched on pieces of birch-bark with a shark's tooth. Then she said, 'Daddy, I've thinked of a secret surprise. You make a noise—any sort of noise.'

'Ah!' said Tegumai. 'Will that do to begin with?'

'Yes,' said Taffy. 'You look just like a carp-fish with its mouth open. Say it again, please.'

'Ah! ah! ah!' said her Daddy. 'Don't be rude, my daughter.'

'I'm not meaning rude, really and truly,' said Taffy. 'It's part of my secret-surprise-think. *Do* say *ah*, Daddy, and keep your mouth open at the end, and lend me that tooth. I'm going to draw a carp-fish's mouth wide-open.'

'What for?' said her Daddy.

'Don't you see?' said Taffy, scratching away on the bark. 'That will be our little secret s'prise. When I draw a carp-fish with his mouth open in the smoke at the back of our Cave—if Mummy doesn't mind—it will remind you of that ah-noise. Then we can play that it was me jumped out of the dark and s'prised you with that noise—same as I did in the beaver-swamp last winter.'

'Really?' said her Daddy, in the voice that grown-ups use when they are truly attending. 'Go on, Taffy.'

'Oh, bother!' she said. 'I can't draw all of a carp-fish, but I can draw something that means a carp-fish's mouth. Don't you know how they stand on their heads rooting in the mud? Well, here's a pretence carp-fish (we can play that the rest of him is drawn). Here's just his mouth, and that means *ah*.' And she drew this.

4

That's not bad,' said Tegumai, and scratched on his own piece of bark for himself; 'but you've forgotten the feeler that hangs across his mouth.'

'But I can't draw, Daddy.'

'You needn't draw anything of him except just the opening of his mouth and the feeler across. Then we'll know he's a carp-fish, 'cause the perches and trouts haven't got feelers. Look here, Taffy.' And he drew this.

'Now I'll copy it,' said Taffy. 'Will you understand *this* when you see it?' And she drew this.

'Perfectly,' said her Daddy. 'And I'll be quite as s'prised when I see it anywhere, as if you had jumped out from behind a tree and said "Ah!"'

6

'Now, make another noise,' said Taffy, very proud.

'Yah!' said her Daddy, very loud.

'H'm,' said Taffy. 'That's a mixy noise. The end part is *ah*-carp-fish-mouth; but what can we do about the front part? *Yer-yer-yer* and *ah! Yah!*'

'It's very like the carp-fish-mouth noise. Let's draw another bit of the carp-fish and join 'em,' said her Daddy. *He* was quite incited too.

'No. If they're joined, I'll forget. Draw it separate. Draw his tail. If he's standing on his head the tail will come first. 'Sides, I think I can draw tails easiest,' said Taffy.

'A good notion,' said Tegumai. 'Here's a carp-fish tail for the *yer*-noise.' And he drew this.

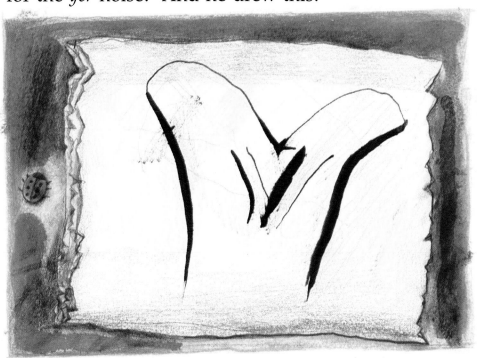

'I'll try now,' said Taffy. ''Member I can't draw like you, Daddy. Will it do if I just draw the split part of the tail, and a sticky-down line for where it joins?' And she drew this.

Her Daddy nodded, and his eyes were shiny bright with 'citement.

'That's beautiful,' she said. 'Now make another noise, Daddy.'

'Oh!' said her Daddy, very loud.

'That's quite easy,' said Taffy. 'You make your mouth all round like an egg or a stone. So an egg or a stone will do for that.'

'You can't always find eggs or stones. We'll have to scratch a round something like one.' And he drew this.

'My gracious!' said Taffy, 'what a lot of noise-pictures we've made,—carp-mouth, carp tail, and egg! Now make another noise, Daddy.'

'Ssh!' said her Daddy, and frowned to himself, but Taffy was too incited to notice.

'That's quite easy,' she said, scratching on the bark.

'Eh, what?' said her Daddy. 'I meant I was thinking, and didn't want to be disturbed.'

'It's a noise, just the same. It's the noise a snake makes, Daddy, when it is thinking and doesn't want to be disturbed. Let's make the *ssh*-noise a snake. Will this do?' And she drew this.

'There,' she said. 'That's another s'prise-secret. When you draw a hissy-snake by the door of your little back-cave where you mend the spears, I'll know you're thinking hard; and I'll come in most mousy-quiet. And if you draw it on a tree by the river when you're fishing, I'll know you want me to walk most *most* mousy-quiet, so as not to shake the banks.'

'Perfectly true,' said Tegumai. 'And there's more in this game than you think. Taffy, dear, I've a notion that your Daddy's daughter has hit upon the finest thing that there ever was since the Tribe of Tegumai took to using shark's teeth instead of flints for their spear-heads. I believe we've found out *the* big secret of the world.'

'Why?' said Taffy, and her eyes shone too with incitement.

'I'll show,' said her Daddy. 'What's water in the Tegumai language?'

'*Ya*, of course, and it means river too—like Wagai-*ya*— the Wagai river.'

9

'What is bad water that gives you fever if you drink it—black water—swamp-water?'

'*Yo*, of course.'

'Now look,' said her Daddy. 'S'pose you saw this scratched by the side of a pool in the beaver-swamp?' And he drew this.

'Carp-tail and round egg. Two noises mixed! *Yo*, bad water,' said Taffy. ''Course I wouldn't drink that water because I'd know you said it was bad.'

'But I needn't be near the water at all. I might be miles away, hunting, and still——'

'And *still* it would be just the same as if you stood there and said, "G'way, Taffy, or you'll get fever." All that in a carp-fish-tail and a round egg! Oh, Daddy, we must tell Mummy, quick!' and Taffy danced all round him.

'Not yet,' said Tegumai; 'not till we've gone a little further. Let's see. *Yo* is bad water, but *so* is food cooked on the fire, isn't it?' And he drew this.

'Yes. Snake and egg,' said Taffy. 'So that means dinner's ready. If you saw that scratched on a tree you'd know it was time to come to the Cave. So'd I.'

'My Winkie!' said Tegumai. 'That's true too. But wait a minute. I see a difficulty. *So* means "come and have dinner," but *sho* means the drying-poles where we hang our hides.'

'Horrid old drying-poles!' said Taffy. 'I hate helping to hang heavy, hot, hairy hides on them. If you drew the snake and egg, and I thought it meant dinner, and I

11

came in from the wood and found that it meant I was to help Mummy hang the hides on the drying-poles, what *would* I do?'

'You'd be cross. So'd Mummy. We must make a new picture for *sho*. We must draw a spotty snake that hisses *sh-sh*, and we'll play that the plain snake only hisses *ssss*.'

'I couldn't be sure how to put in the spots,' said Taffy. 'And p'raps if *you* were in a hurry you might leave them out, and I'd think it was *so* when it was *sho*, and then Mummy would catch me just the same. *No!* I think we'd better draw a picture of the horrid high drying-poles their very selves, and make *quite* sure. I'll put 'em in just after the hissy-snake. Look!' And she drew this.   *SHO*

'P'raps that's safest. It's very like our drying-poles, anyhow,' said her Daddy, laughing. 'Now I'll make a new noise with a snake and drying-pole sound in it. I'll say *shi*. That's Tegumai for spear, Taffy.' And he laughed.

'Don't make fun of me,' said Taffy, as she thought of her picture-letter and the mud in the Stranger-man's hair. '*You* draw it, Daddy.'

'We won't have beavers or hills this time, eh?' said her Daddy. 'I'll just draw a straight   *SHI* line for my spear.' And he drew this.

'Even Mummy couldn't mistake that for me being killed.'

'*Please* don't, Daddy. It makes me uncomfy. Do some more noises. We're getting on beautifully.'

'Er-hm!' said Tegumai, looking up. 'We'll say *shu*. That means sky.'

Taffy drew the snake and the drying-pole. Then she stopped. 'We must make a new picture for that end sound, mustn't we?'

'*Shu-shu-u-u-u!*' said her Daddy. 'Why, it's just like the round-egg-sound made thin.'

'Then s'pose we draw a thin round egg, and pretend it's a frog that hasn't eaten anything for years.'

'N-no,' said her Daddy. 'If we drew that in a hurry we might mistake it for the round egg itself. *Shu-shu-shu!* I'll tell you what we'll do. We'll open a little hole at the end of the round egg to show how the O-noise runs out all thin, *ooo-oo-oo*. Like this.' And he drew this.

'Oh, that's lovely! Much better than a thin frog. Go on,' said Taffy, using her shark's tooth.

Her Daddy went on drawing, and his hand shook with incitement. He went on till he had drawn this.

'Don't look up, Taffy,' he said. 'Try if you can make out what that means in the Tegumai language. If you can, we've found the Secret.'

'Snake—pole—broken-egg—carp-tail and carp-mouth,' said Taffy. '*Shu-ya*. Sky-water [rain].' Just then a drop fell on her hand, for the day had clouded over. 'Why, Daddy, it's raining. Was *that* what you meant to tell me?'

'Of course,' said her Daddy. 'And I told it you without saying a word, didn't I?'

'Well, I *think* I would have known it in a minute, but that raindrop made me quite sure. I'll always remember now. *Shu-ya* means rain, or "it is going to rain." Why, Daddy!' She got up and danced round him. 'S'pose you went out before I was awake, and drawed *shu-ya* in the smoke on the wall, I'd know it was going to rain and I'd take my beaver-skin hood. Wouldn't Mummy be s'prised!'

Tegumai got up and danced. (Daddies didn't mind doing those things in those days.) 'More than that! More than that!' he said. 'S'pose I wanted to tell you it wasn't going to rain much and you must come down to the river, what would we draw? Say the words in Tegumai-talk first.'

'*Shu-ya-las, ya maru*. [Sky-water ending. River come to.] *What* a lot of new sounds! *I* don't see how we can draw them.'

15

'But I do—but I do!' said Tegumai. 'Just attend a minute, Taffy, and we won't do any more to-day. We've got *shu-ya* all right, haven't we? but this *las* is a teaser. *La-la-la!*' and he waved his shark-tooth.

'There's the hissy-snake at the end and the carp-mouth before the snake—*as-as-as*. We only want *la-la*,' said Taffy.

'I know it, but we have to make *la-la*. And we're the first people in all the world who've ever tried to do it, Taffimai!'

'Well,' said Taffy, yawning, for she was rather tired. '*Las* means breaking or finishing as well as ending, doesn't it?'

'So it does,' said Tegumai. *Ya-las* means that there's no water in the tank for Mummy to cook with—just when I'm going hunting, too.'

'And *shi-las* means that your spear is broken. If I'd only thought of *that* instead of drawing silly beaver-pictures for the Stranger-man!'

'La! La! La!' said Tegumai, waving his stick and frowning. 'Oh, bother!'

'I could have drawn *shi* quite easily,' Taffy went on. 'Then I'd have drawn your spear all broken—this way!' And she drew.

'The very thing,' said Tegumai. 'That's *la* all over. It isn't like any of the other marks, either.' And he drew this.

'Now for *ya*. Oh, we've done that before. Now for *maru*. *Mum-mum-mum*. *Mum* shuts one's mouth up, doesn't it? We'll draw a shut mouth like this.' And he drew.

17

'Then the carp-mouth open. That makes *Ma-ma-ma*! But what about this *rrrrr*-thing, Taffy?'

'It sounds all rough and edgy, like your shark-tooth saw when you're cutting out a plank for the canoe,' said Taffy.

'You mean all sharp at the edges, like this?' said Tegumai. And he drew.

''Xactly,' said Taffy. 'But we don't want all those teeth: only put two.'

'I'll only put in one,' said Tegumai. 'If this game of ours is going to be what I think it will, the easier we make our sound-pictures the better for everybody.' And he drew.

'*Now* we've got it,' said Tegumai, standing on one leg. 'I'll draw 'em all in a string like fish.'

'Hadn't we better put a little bit of stick or something between each word, so's they won't rub up against each other and jostle, same as if they were carps?'

'Oh, I'll leave a space for that,' said her Daddy. And very incitedly he drew them all without stopping, on a big new bit of birch-bark.

'*Shu-ya-las-ya-maru*,' said Taffy, reading it out sound by sound.

'That's enough for to-day,' said Tegumai. 'Besides, you're getting tired, Taffy. Never mind, dear. We'll finish it all to-morrow, and then we'll be remembered for years and years after the biggest trees you can see are all chopped up for firewood.'

So they went home, and all that evening Tegumai sat

on one side of the fire and Taffy on the other, drawing *ya's* and *yo's* and *shu's* and *shi's* in the smoke on the wall and giggling together till her Mummy said, 'Really, Tegumai, you're worse than my Taffy.'

'Please don't mind,' said Taffy. It's only our secret-s'prise Mummy, dear, and we'll tell you all about it the very minute it's done; but *please* don't ask me what it is now, or else I'll have to tell.'

So her Mummy most carefully didn't; and bright and early next morning Tegumai went down to the river to think about new sound-pictures, and when Taffy got up she saw *Ya-las* [water is ending or running out] chalked on the side of the big stone water-tank, outside the Cave.

'Um,' said Taffy. 'These picture-sounds are rather a bother! Daddy's just as good as come here himself and told me to get more water for Mummy to cook with.' She went to the spring at the back of the Cave and filled the tank from a bark bucket, and then she ran down to the river and pulled her Daddy's left ear—the one that belonged to her to pull when she was good.

'Now come along and we'll draw all the left-over sound-pictures,' said her Daddy, and they had a most inciting day of it, and a beautiful lunch in the middle, and two games of romps. When they came to T, Taffy said that as her name, and her Daddy's, and her Mummy's all began with that sound, they should draw a sort of family group of themselves holding hands. That

was all very well to draw once or twice; but when it came to drawing it six or seven times, Taffy and Tegumai drew it scratchier and scratchier, till at last the T-sound was only a thin long Tegumai with his arms out to hold Taffy and Teshumai. You can see from these three pictures partly how it happened.

Many of the other pictures were much too beautiful to begin with, especially before lunch; but as they were drawn over and over again on birch-bark, they became plainer and easier, till at last even Tegumai said he could find no fault with them. They turned the hissy-snake the other way round for the Z-sound, to show it was hissing backwards in a soft and gentle way; and they just made a twiddle for E, because it came into the pictures so often;

and they drew pictures of the sacred Beaver of the Tegumais for the B-sound;

and because it was a nasty, nosy noise, they just drew noses for the N-sound, till they were tired;

and they drew a picture of the big lake-pike's mouth for the greedy Ga-sound; and they drew the pike's mouth again with a spear behind it for the scratchy, hurty Ka-sound; and they drew pictures of a little bit of the winding Wagai river for the nice windy-windy Wa-sound;

and so on and so forth and so following till they had done and drawn all the sound-pictures that they wanted, and there was the Alphabet, all complete.

And after thousands and thousands and thousands of years, and after Hieroglyphics, and Demotics, and Nilotics, and Cryptics, and Cufics, and Runics, and Dorics, and Ionics, and all sorts of other ricks and tricks (because the Woons, and the Neguses, and the Akhoonds, and the Repositories of Tradition would never leave a good thing alone when they saw it), the fine old easy, understandable Alphabet—A, B, C, D, E, and the rest of 'em—got back into its proper shape again for all Best Beloveds to learn when they are old enough.

But *I* remember Tegumai Bopsulai, and Taffimai Metallumai, and Teshumai Tewindrow, her dear Mummy, and all the days gone by. And it was so—just so—a long time ago—on the banks of the big Wagai!

ONE of the first things that Tegumai Bopsulai did after Taffy and he had made the Alphabet was to make a magic Alphabet-necklace of all the letters, so that it could be put in the Temple of Tegumai and kept for ever and ever. All the Tribe of Tegumai brought their most precious beads and beautiful things, and Taffy and Tegumai spent five whole years getting the necklace in order. This is a picture of the magic Alphabet-necklace. The string was made of the finest and strongest reindeer-sinew, bound round with thin copper wire.

Beginning at the top, the first bead is an old silver one that belonged to the Head Priest of the Tribe of Tegumai; then come three black mussel-pearls; next is a clay bead (blue and grey); next a nubbly gold bead sent as a present by a tribe who got it from Africa (but it must have been Indian really); the next is a long flat-sided glass bead from Africa (the Tribe of Tegumai took it in a fight); then come two clay beads (white and green), with dots on one, and dots and bands on the other; next are three rather chipped amber beads; then three clay beads (red and white), two with dots, and the big one in the middle with a toothed pattern. Then the letters begin, and between each letter is a little whitish clay bead with the letter repeated small. Here are the letters:—

A is scratched on a tooth—an elk-tush, I think.

B is the Sacred Beaver of Tegumai on a bit of old ivory.

C is a pearly oyster-shell—inside front.

D must be a sort of mussel-shell—outside front.

E is a twist of silver wire.

F is broken, but what remains of it is a bit of stag's horn.

G is painted black on a piece of wood. (The bead after G is a small shell, and not a clay bead. I don't know why they did that.)

H is a kind of big brown cowrie-shell.

I is the inside part of a long shell ground down by hand. (It took Tegumai three months to grind it down.)

J is a fish-hook in mother-of-pearl.

L is the broken spear in silver. (K ought to follow J, of course; but the necklace was broken once and they mended it wrong.)

K is a thin slice of bone scratched and rubbed in black.

M is on a pale grey shell.

N is a piece of what is called porphyry with a nose scratched on it. (Tegumai spent five months polishing this stone.)

O is a piece of oyster-shell with a hole in the middle.

P and Q are missing. They were lost, a long time ago, in a great war, and the tribe mended the necklace with the dried rattles of a rattlesnake, but no one ever found P and Q. That is how the saying began, 'You must mind your P's and Q's.

R is, of course, just a shark's tooth.

S is a little silver snake.

T is the end of a small bone, polished brown and shiny.

U is another piece of oyster-shell.

W is a twisty piece of mother-of-pearl that they found inside a big mother-of-pearl shell, and sawed off with a wire dipped in sand and water. It took Taffy a month and a half to polish it and drill the holes.

X is silver wire joined in the middle with a raw garnet.
(Taffy found the garnet.)

Y is the carp's tail in ivory.

Z is a bell-shaped piece of agate marked with Z-shaped
stripes. They made the Z-snake out of one of the
stripes by picking out the soft stone and rubbing in red
sand and beeswax. Just in the mouth of the bell you
see the clay bead repeating the Z-letter.

These are all the letters.

The next bead is a small round greeny lump of copper ore;
the next is a lump of rough turquoise; the next is a rough gold
nugget (what they call water-gold); the next is a melon-
shaped clay bead (white with green spots). Then come four
flat ivory pieces, with dots on them rather like dominoes; then
come three stone beads, very badly worn; then two soft iron
beads with rust-holes at the edges (they must have been
magic, because they look very common); and last is a very
very old African bead, like glass—blue, red, white, black, and
yellow. Then comes the loop to slip over the big silver button
at the other end, and that is all.

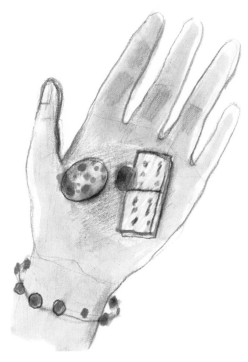

I have copied the necklace very carefully. It weighs one pound seven and a half ounces. The black squiggle behind is only put in to make the beads and things look better.

Of all the Tribe of Tegumai
    Who cut that figure, none remain,—
On Merrow Down the cuckoos cry—
    The silence and the sun remain.

But as the faithful years return
    And hearts unwounded sing again,
Comes Taffy dancing through the fern
    To lead the Surrey spring again.

Her brows are bound with bracken-fronds,
    And golden elf-locks fly above;
Her eyes are bright as diamonds
    And bluer than the sky above.

In moccasins and deer-skin cloak,
    Unfearing, free and fair she flits,
And lights her little damp-wood smoke
    To show her Daddy where she flits.

For far—oh, very far behind,
    So far she cannot call to him,
Comes Tegumai alone to find
    The daughter that was all to him.

A B C D E
F G H I J K
L M N O
P Q R S
T U V W
X Y Z

#90-19

E   Kipling, Rudyard
Kip
          How the alphabet was
          made